CAPTAIN UNDERPANTS
AND THE BIG, BAD BATTLE OF THE BIONIC BOOGER BOY
PART 2: THE REVENGE OF THE RIDICULOUS ROBO-BOOGERS

The Seventh Epic Novel by

DAV PILKEY

SCHOLASTIC INC.
New York Toronto London Auckland Sydney
Mexico City New Delhi Hong Kong Buenos Aires

This book is being published simultaneously in hardcover by the Blue Sky Press.

ISBN 0-439-37612-2

Be sure to check out Dav Pilkey's Extra-Crunchy Web Site O' Fun at
www.pilkey.com.

12 11 10 9 8 7 6 5 4 3 2   3 4 5 6 7 8/0

Printed in the United States of America   40

First Scholastic paperback printing, October 2003

FOR AIDAN AND AUDREY HAMLIN

CHAPTERS

The Sad, Sad Truth About CAPTAIN UNDERPants

Onse upon a time there were two cool kids named George and Harold.

Wer'e MecHa-Groovy

Me Too.

But Unforch-enetly they had a mean Prinsipel named Mr. Krupp.

BLaH BLaH BLaH

So one day they hipnotized him with a 3-D Hypno ring.

you will obey our every command.

Yes Masters.

Mr. Krupp Became under their control.

You are now a monkey.

HAHaHa!

O-O-O

But they made a TERIBEL MISTAKE

You are now captain underpants

OK

HA HA HA HA

TRA-LA-LAAAA!

It was FUNNY until he jumped out ~~of~~ the window.

Hey Come Back Here!

No way

Mr. Krupp really thout he was ~~to~~ a real superhero. He got in all kinds of Trouble.

oh no!

One time he almost got killed by a dandyLion.

Help!

So George stole some Super Power Juice from a U.F.O.

and he gave it to him.

super power Juice

glub
glub
glub

and ~~Capta~~ Mr. Krupp got Super Powers.

Now he can fly and stuff.

Here we go again

Now whenever MR. Krupp hears sombody snap there fingers....

BLah BLah BLah!!!

SNAP

... he TURNS into Captain Underpants.

Tra-La-Laaa!

And whenever C.U. gets water on his head...

H2O

he turns back into MR. Krupp.

BLah BLah BLah!

So Remember!!! Don't snap your fingers around Mr. Krupp!

BUT...

Thats only THE FIRST PART of OUR STORY......

READ ON!

OK. Well there's is this other kid in our sckool named Melvin Sneedly.

Im a DUMB nerd.

Melvin invented a combine-o-thingy that morfs stuff together.

First he combined his pet hamster (sulu) with a robot.

Sulu   Robot

Youreeka!!! I have created the worlds first Bionic hamster.

Next he tried to combine himself with a robot...

But he Sneezed at the Last second.

A-A-CHOO!

And he axidentelly got combined with a ROBOT--- And his Boogers!

ZAP!

He Became the Bionic Booger Boy.

I'm a DUMB Nerd!

UH OH

Then one time he coght a cold.

A-CHOO

Then he got mad and Terned into a monster.

Then he ate up Captain Underpants.

But Sulu The Bionic Hamster Beat him up.

Then Melvins Parents came and Reversed the comBin-o-Thingy.

They zapped him and BLEW away The Boogers.

ZAP

BOOM

Now Melvin and Mr. KRUPP were safe.

But somthing was wrong with them.

Im a DUMB Nerd

BLAH BLAH BLAH!

Then The Boogers came to Life and smashed the combine-o-thingy...

CRASH!

... And the chase was on!!!

THE END... OF PART 1

CHAPTER 1

GEORGE AND HAROLD

This is George Beard and Harold Hutchins. George is the kid on the left with the tie and the flat-top. Harold is the one on the right with the T-shirt and the bad haircut. Remember that now.

This is Mr. Krupp, Melvin Sneedly, and Sulu the Bionic Hamster. Mr. Krupp is the one on the left with the underwear and the bald head. Melvin is the one on the right with the bow tie and the glasses. And Sulu the Bionic Hamster is the hamstery-looking one in the middle with the laser eyeballs,

the Macro-Hydraulic Jump-A-Tronic legs, the Super-Somgobulating mini-Automo-Arms, the virtually indestructible Flexo-Growmonic endoskeleton, and the Twin Turbo-3000 SP5 Kung-Fu Titanium/Lithium Alloy Processor. Remember that now, too.

And these are the Ridiculous Robo-
Boogers. Three of the vilest, most disgusting,
and most terrifying creatures ever to drip
across the face of the Earth. Even their
names were horrible, monstrous monikers,
the sound of which would drive madness
into the hearts of the bravest of heroes.

If you dare to know their nightmarishly deplorable names, I will tell you. But don't blame me if you have to sleep with a night-light on for the rest of your life.

Their names were (from left to right) Carl, Trixie, and Frankenbooger.

See? I told you they were scary names!

Carl, Trixie, and Frankenbooger each bellowed out terrifying, ear-piercing screams of unstoppable fury as they chased our heroes down the city streets. Finally, the Robo-Boogers cornered everyone in a dead-end alley. The three phlegmish fiends oozed closer and closer, until at last they leaped toward their prey.

The situation had become so frightening that George, Harold, Melvin, and Mr. Krupp closed their eyes tightly and waited for the terrifying sounds of their own inevitable demise.

GLoBBle! GLoBBle! GLoBBle!

But instead of hearing inevitable-demisey-type sounds, our heroes heard something quite diferent. You see, at the very last second, Sulu the Bionic Hamster stretched open his Flexo-Growmonic jaw and shoved the three boogery behemoths into his mouth.

Sulu's bionic cheeks swelled to capacity as he raised his furry head toward the sky.

Then, with the force of a lunar shuttle liftoff, Sulu shot the three slimy villains into space.

SPIT-TOOIE! SPIT-TOOIE! SPIT-TOOIE!

The three Ridiculous Robo-Boogers sailed through the sky like cannonballs. In no time at all, they left Earth's atmosphere and began sailing toward Uranus. The terrifying battle was over.

"Wow, that was a really quick story," said Harold. "This is going to be our shortest adventure ever!"

"Ain't *that* the truth!" said George.

CHAPTER 2
IT AIN'T

Unfortunately for George and Harold, their adventure had only just begun. As everyone walked back to school, a confusing argument got underway.

"I want my hamster back," said Mr. Krupp.

"*Your* hamster?" said George. "First of all, he's *OUR* hamster now. And second of all, he never belonged to you. He belonged to Melvin."

"I don't care WHO he belongs to," Melvin interrupted. "Hamsters aren't allowed in school . . . especially not in MY SCHOOL! I'm giving all three of you bubs a detention for bringing that furry beast into your classroom!"

"You can't give us a detention," said Harold. "You're just a kid like us!"

Suddenly, Mr. and Mrs. Sneedly came running toward them.

"Melvin, you're alright!" cried Mrs. Sneedly.

"We're so happy you're safe, son!" cried Mr. Sneedly.

"Mommy! Poppa!" cried Mr. Krupp. He dashed over to Melvin's parents with open arms. The sight of a bald, grown man in his underwear running toward them made Mrs. Sneedly scream in horror.

"Hey, what's the big idea?" yelled Mr. Sneedly.

"It's me, Poppa," cried Mr. Krupp. "Don't you recognize your own son?"

"Get away from us, you—you—you
WEIRDO!" Mrs. Sneedly yelled as she hit
Mr. Krupp with her purse.

Melvin ignored the commotion as he
walked past them all and went into
the school.

Melvin stormed upstairs and headed for the school office. Everyone except Miss Anthrope had already gone home for the day, and she was getting ready to leave, too.

"Just where do you think you're going, woman?!!?" shouted Melvin.

Miss Anthrope turned and stared in shock at the fourth grader standing behind her.

"What did you JUST *SAY*?!!?" she cried
in a voice that was rapidly becoming a
scream. "Who—WHO DO YOU THINK
YOU ARE?!!?"

"I'm the guy who's gonna fire your hiney
if you don't get me my coffee . . . *NOW*!"
yelled Melvin.

Normally, school secretaries don't have the authority to hang a child from a coat hook by his underwear, but today had been a particularly stressful day for Miss Anthrope. She had been covered in snot, carried through town by a rampaging robotic monster, and (worst of all) forced to chaperone an elementary school field trip. Now it was payback time.

CHAPTER 3

MR. MELVIN AND KRUPPY THE KID

Miss Anthrope collected her things and left for home, grumbling under her breath as she passed George and Harold in the hallway. The two boys could hear Melvin's angry shouts coming from down the hall, so they went to the office to investigate.

   While they were getting Melvin off the
hook, Mr. Krupp ran into the office, sweaty
and out of breath.

   "You guys have gotta help me," he cried.
"My mom and dad are trying to kill me! Has
the world gone MAD?"

   "Relax, Einstein," said George calmly,
"and put on some clothes!" George and
Harold had already figured out what was
going on, so they tried to explain the
situation to Melvin and Mr. Krupp.

"You see," said Harold, "after you guys got morphed together by the Combine-O-Tron 2000, we switched the batteries around and separated you. But for some strange reason, it switched your *brains* around. Now Mr. Krupp's brain is inside Melvin's body, and Melvin's brain is inside Mr. Krupp's body."

"That's a buncha BUNK!" yelled Melvin.

"Take a look and see for yourselves," said
George. He pulled a full-length mirror in
front of Mr. Krupp and Melvin. They looked
at themselves in astonishment.

"I'm—I'm a kid again," said the guy who
looked like Melvin but had Mr. Krupp's brain.

"And I'm old and fat and bald and ugly,"
cried the guy who looked like Mr. Krupp but
had Melvin's brain. "And I have bad breath
and creepy nose hairs and—"

"HEY!" yelled the guy who looked like
Melvin but had Mr. Krupp's brain.

At this point, you might be saying to yourself, "Dang, this book is getting confusing!" Now don't worry, this'll all get cleared up by the end of chapter 17. But for now, let's rename the two characters who have the right brains in the wrong bodies, shall we? Let's call the guy who looks like Mr. Krupp (but has Melvin Sneedly's brain) "Mr. Melvin." And we'll call the kid who looks like Melvin Sneedly (but has Mr. Krupp's brain) "Kruppy the Kid."

Please refer to the handy X-ray chart below in case you get mixed-up:

MELVIN'S BRAIN

MR. KRUPP'S BRAIN

MR. MELVIN

KRUPPY the KID

CHAPTER 4
THINGS GET WORSE

Kruppy the Kid climbed up into his chair and demanded to know what was going to be done about this mix-up.

"I could solve this problem right away if I still had my Combine-O-Tron 2000," said Mr. Melvin sheepishly, "but it got smashed in the last book."

"Well start building a new one, bub!" shouted Kruppy the Kid.

"O.K.," whined Mr. Melvin, "but it'll take about six months."

"SIX MONTHS?!!?" screamed Kruppy the Kid. "I can't go around looking like a kid for six months! I've got a school to run, buster!"

"Sorry," Mr. Melvin whimpered, "but building a cellular combiner is extremely difficult. It takes time. It's not easy like building a robot, or a time machine, or a Photo-Atomic Trans-Somgobulating Yectofantriplutoniczanziptomiser."

"Hey, wait a second," said George. "Did you just say that building a time machine was *easy*?"

"Yeah," said Mr. Melvin. "It just takes a day or two. Why?"

"Well, why don't you just build a time machine?" asked George. "Then you can go back in time to before the Combine-O-Tron 2000 got smashed, grab it, and bring it back to the present time."

Mr. Melvin thought for a moment, and then his eyes lit up. "I've got it!" he said, snapping his fingers. "I'll build a time machine, then go back in time to before the Combine-O-Tron 2000 got smashed, grab it, and bring it back to the—hey, what the heck is *HE* doing?!!?"

Everyone turned and looked at Kruppy
the Kid, who had just stripped down to his
underwear and was now tying a red curtain
around his neck.

"OH, NO!" screamed George. "GET SOME
WATER!!! GET SOME WATER!!!"

Harold ran out to the drinking fountain,
but he was too late. Kruppy the Kid shouted
a triumphant "Tra-La-Laaaaa!", then turned
and flew out the window.

CHAPTER 5
THINGS GET WORSER

"Did—did you guys just see that?" cried Mr. Melvin. "I just—I mean, Kruppy the Kid just flew out the window! He FLEW!"

"Yeah, we know," said George with a sigh.

"That's—that's *amazing*!" cried Mr. Melvin. "He must think he's Captain Underpants or something. Or . . . or could it be? Could our principal really BE Captain Underpants?"

"Well, *duh*!" said Harold.

"But Mr. Krupp doesn't look anything like Captain Underpants," said Mr. Melvin frantically. "Captain Underpants is bald! And Mr. Krupp usually has hair. Hey! I know! Maybe Mr. Krupp wears a toupee?"

"I thought you were supposed to be in the 'gifted' program," said George.

"But—but how can he fly? Where did he get his super powers?" asked Mr. Melvin.

"It's a long story," said Harold.

Mr. Melvin calmed down a bit, walked confidently across the room, and sat in the principal's chair. He leaned back and smiled a devilish grin. "Well, why don't you go ahead and tell me all about it?" said Mr. Melvin. "I've got all the time in the world!"

CHAPTER 6

THINGS GET WORSEREST

George and Harold had no choice but to come clean. They told Mr. Melvin the whole story of Captain Underpants: how they had hypnotized Mr. Krupp, how he drank the alien Super Power Juice, and how his super powers must have somehow gotten transferred into Melvin's body along with Mr. Krupp's brain.

While George and Harold were talking, the smile on Mr. Melvin's face grew wider and wider, and eviler and eviler.

"What're you smiling about?" said George. "This is SERIOUS!"

"Yeah," said Harold. "We're all in big trouble if we don't switch things back to normal!"

"Correction," said Mr. Melvin. "*YOU* guys are in big trouble. All my troubles are OVER. I, Melvin Sneedly, am gonna get back into my old body, but KEEP those super powers for myself. I'm gonna become the world's first super-powered kid!"

"Hey, you can't do that," said Harold.

"I can do whatever I want," snapped Mr. Melvin. "I'm in charge now. I look just like the principal, so I'm gonna make the rules, and you guys are gonna follow them—or else!"

"Or else what?" George demanded.

"Or *else*," snarled Mr. Melvin, "I'll order your teachers to give you guys twelve hours of homework every night for the next eight years!"

That shut George and Harold up.

Mr. Melvin's first order of the day was for George and Harold to make a new comic book about the world's first super-powered kid, Melvin Sneedly.

"Give me a really cool name," said Mr. Melvin, "like *Big Melvin* or *Mystery Melvin* . . ."

"MYSTERY MELVIN???" said George and Harold in disbelief.

". . . and make up a story where I defeat Captain Underpants and become the world's greatest superhero. And you better not make me look stupid, either!" Mr. Melvin shouted.

"But we can't make a comic book right now," cried Harold. "We've gotta chase after Captain Kruppy the . . . uh . . . Underpants Kid."

"You can chase after him all you want," said Mr. Melvin, "*AFTER* you make that comic book. Now get going! I've got a time machine to build."

CHAPTER 7
THE PURPLE POTTY

Mr. Melvin went out and bought all the things he needed to build his time machine. Now he just needed a *place* to build it. He wanted someplace quiet and private. Someplace empty and secluded. A room that nobody ever, EVER used.

"I've got it!" he cried. "Our school library!"

The library at Jerome Horwitz Elementary
School had once been a wonderful place
of knowledge and learning. But a few years
back, the librarian, Miss Singerbrains, had
begun banning most of the books. Now
the library was filled only with rows of empty
bookshelves and posters that warned of
the potential subversive dangers of reading.
It was the perfect place to hatch an evil plan.

Mr. Melvin pushed his cart into the dusty,
cobwebby room and flicked on the lights.

"Welcome, sir," said Miss Singerbrains. "Have you come to check out the book?"

"Uh, nooo," said Mr. Melvin. "I need to find a large box, like a phone booth or something."

"There's a purple portable potty down in the basement," said Miss Singerbrains.

"That'll do," Mr. Melvin said. "Go get it for me."

"I can't carry that thing up three flights of stairs all by myself," cried Miss Singerbrains.

"Alright, alright," said Mr. Melvin. "I'll help you."

Mr. Melvin supervised while Miss
Singerbrains carried the heavy potty
to the top of the treacherous steps.

"Good job," said Mr. Melvin. "Now go
clean out your desk. You're fired."

"*FIRED?!!?*" cried Miss Singerbrains.
"What for?"

"Uh . . . for the rest of your life," said
Mr. Melvin.

CHAPTER 8

MEANWHILE, BACK IN OUTER SPACE . . .

A team of scientists working at the Piqua
Order of Professional Space and Interplanetary
Explorers (POOPSIE) were on their way to
investigate the planet Uranus, when they
came across something that was very strange.

Major "Buzz" Tomski and his crew had just discovered a bizarre cluster of what appeared to be robots and toilets resting on the planet's surface.

The astronauts were so busy looking at their monitor that they didn't notice the three slimy, squishy, boogery thingies speeding toward their spaceship.

CHAPTER 9

GROUND CONTROL TO MAJOR TOMSKI

Suddenly, a very concerned voice came across the POOPSIE space phone. "What's going on up there, bub?" asked Ground Control.

"W-we're O.K.," said Major Tomski as he unzipped the cockpit's window screen for a better look. "But it appears our ship has just been splattered by three unidentified squishy objects!"

"That does it!" said Ground Control. "This mission is just getting too strange. I want you guys to turn that ship around and come on back home."

"Will do," said Major Tomski. He pushed in the clutch, shifted the ship into reverse, and in no time at all, the POOPSIE shuttle was headed back to Earth . . .

. . . with three giggling stowaways hanging
on for the long ride home.

CHAPTER 10

MEAN MR. MELVIN

The next day, Mr. Melvin was putting the
finishing touches on his time machine when
he heard cries of laughter out in the hallway.

He opened the library door and saw a
group of third graders happily reading
George and Harold's newest comic book.
Mr. Melvin stomped down the hall, grabbed
the comic out of their hands, and gasped
in horror.

"WHAT THE—?!!?" he screamed as he
glared at the comic book's cover.

CHAPTER 11

Captain Underpants

AND THE WAR OF THE WILEY WONDER NERD

a Gripping Tale of Action and Horror

By George Beard and Harold Hutch,

Onse upon a time there was a new-clear Power Plant.

It had a Lots of waste.

newclear waste removal

The Waste was ~~the~~ supost to Be Taken to a dump...

newclear waste removal

... But one barral ~~slipped~~ fell off.

Newc WAST Remor

The Barral rolled down a hill...

and Landed in a Cotten Feild.

GLug glug glug

Soon the cotten soaked up the new-clear waste and began to grow.

Then one Time the Cotten got Harvested

This cotten Balls shure is Heavy.

Yeah, its Big to!

cotten

And they took it to the Underwear Facktory.

BUB's Underwear Facktory

Tims Cotten

The Cotton got made into Underwear.

Hey its glowing

Soon....

Look Melvin Theres is a sale on glow in-the-dark underwear!

Duh me want some mommy Duh.

Soon Melvin had his very own pair.

Now your the coolest kid ever.

Duh I shure am.

But that night the Radioactive Underwear made him grow.

DOLLYS are COOL

I ♥ Unicorns

DOLLY DREAM HOUSE

and Grow...

... and grow...

Melvins House

CRASH

The next morning Melvin woke up.

YAWN

CRASH

So he walked to school.

DUH I'm Grum-py

Boom

Boom Boom

Boom

Sir a giant nerd is atacking the city.

Call the army and stuff

soon the army and stuff arived.

Then there was a Big war.

I'm telling

Wonder Nerd Picked up a tank and Threw it.

MMMF

meanwhile at a nearby sckool...

You guys are pathetick!

Your worthless and weak!

Gym

CRASH

Help! Wonder Nerd just Threw a Tank and Squished Sombody!!!

OH NO!!! who was it?

Prinsiple

The gym Teacher.

Thank Goodness!!! I Thout it was Sombody important!

Prinsiple

This Looks Like a Job For...

CAPTAIN UNDERPANTS

"Hey wonder nerd, Quit it!"

"I'm not a nerd. I'm cool!!! My mommy said so!"

Captain underpants flew around and saw a tag on wonder Nerds Undies.

Warning: this underpants may shrink when washed.

"Hmmm."

HORAY FOR Captain UNDERPANTS!

PRINCIPAL

waaaa!

ITS OFF TO Nerd JAIL For you!

TRA-LA LAAAA

Jail For DUMB STU-PID nerds.

T
EN

moreL :

always BUY PRE-SHRUNK underwears

Treehouse Comix Inc.

CHAPTER 12
MAD MR. MELVIN

Mr. Melvin was furious. He marched into the office and turned on the school intercom.

"George Beard and Harold Hutchins," he shouted over the loudspeakers, "meet Mr. Melv—er, I mean, Mr. *Krupp* in the school library RIGHT NOW!"

"We have a library?" said George.

After about twenty minutes of searching, George and Harold finally came across a room they had never seen before. They entered cautiously, stepping quietly past rows and rows of empty bookshelves until they met up with Mr. Melvin.

"I told you guys to give me a cool name and not to make me look stupid!" Mr. Melvin screamed, clutching their comic book in his sweaty hand.

"Oops," said George. "I thought you said to give you a stupid name and NOT to make you look cool."

"Yeah," said Harold. "It was an honest misunderstanding."

Mr. Melvin threw the comic book to the ground, then led George and Harold over to the Purple Potty.

"Remember when I had that great idea to build a time machine?" asked Mr. Melvin.

"Actually," said George, "that was *my*—"

"Well, here it is," Mr. Melvin interrupted triumphantly. "And you two smarty-pantses are going to test it out for me!"

"Huh?" said Harold.

"I'm sending you kids back in time to the day before yesterday," Mr. Melvin said. "And you better not return until you've got my Combine-O-Tron 2000."

"Cool," said George. "I've always wanted to travel through time."

Mr. Melvin had a great deal of instructions for George and Harold before they left on their journey. And though the instructions were quite boring, it would have benefited the boys if they had paid attention instead of switching the letters around on a nearby bulletin board.

Mr. Melvin spoke at length about the workings of the time machine and the proper etiquette of time travel.

"You must be very careful that nobody sees you on your journey," Mr. Melvin said. "If they do, just zap them with my new invention, the Forgetchamacallit 2000."

"This will erase everything in their short-term memory, and they won't remember ever seeing you." Mr. Melvin had also built a fake Combine-O-Tron 2000 to switch with the real one.

Finally, Mr. Melvin gave George and Harold a very important warning: "Whatever you do, it is very important that you don't use this time machine two days in a row. It needs to cool off *every other day*, or else it might open up an oppozo-dimensional reality rift that could destroy the entire planet."

George and Harold started laughing at their new message on the bulletin board.

"HEY!" Mr. Melvin shouted. "Have you kids even heard *one* word I've said?"

"Yeah, yeah, yeah," said George. "We gotta switch the thing with the thingy!"

"And if somebody sees us," said Harold, "we'll zap 'em with the whichamajiggy."

"Don't worry, we *got* it!" said George.

George and Harold stepped into the Purple Potty as Mr. Melvin closed the door behind them. Harold set the controller for the day before yesterday. Then George pulled the chain. Suddenly, there was a brilliant flash of green light, and the Purple Potty disappeared.

CHAPTER 13

THE DAY BEFORE YESTERDAY

After a few moments of flashing lights, everything became quiet. Harold opened the potty
door and peeked out into the darkened
library. Cautiously the two time travelers
stepped to the library window and looked
out. There they saw Melvin's father, Mr.
Sneedly, zapping the Bionic Booger Boy with
a blast from the Combine-O-Tron 2000.

"Been there," said George.

"Done that," said Harold.

In the corner, George and Harold found a coat and hat, which belonged to Miss Singerbrains. Immediately, they thought of a plan. Harold put on the coat and hat, and climbed onto George's shoulders.

"I sure hope this disguise works," said Harold.

"It better," said George. "We can't risk letting them recognize us."

Soon George and Harold were at the scene of the action. Mr. Sneedly had just fired the Combine-O-Tron 2000 a second time, and now the boys were ready to make their move.

"Um, excuse me, Mr. Sneedly," said Harold, trying very hard to sound like a grown-up. "I'd like to present unto you *The Most Brilliantest Science Guy of the Whole Wide World Award.*"

"Really?" cried Mr. Sneedly. "It's always been my dream to win that award!"

"But first," said Harold, "I'd like to have a look at that Combine-O-Thingy."

"O.K.," said Mr. Sneedly. He handed Harold the Combine-O-Tron 2000 and smiled proudly.

"Um . . . " said Harold. "I need to look at it behind those bushes over there."

Harold and George wobbled over to the bushes, unbuttoned their coat, and switched the two Combine-O-Trons. Then they wobbled back and handed the fake Combine-O-Tron 2000 to Mr. Sneedly.

"Um . . . everything seems to be in order," said Harold. "But before we present the award, we'd like to get a photo of you."

"Who's *we*?" asked Mr. Sneedly.

"Uh . . . I mean *I'd* like to get a photo of you," said Harold nervously.

George stuck his hand out of the coat and held up the Forgetchamacallit 2000.

"Say cheese," said Harold.

Mr. Sneedly looked down in shock at George's hand. Then George pressed the button.

FLASH!

Suddenly, Mr. Sneedly forgot everything
that had just happened. Dazed and confused,
he stumbled back and rejoined his wife just
in time for the Robo-Boogers to come to life
and smash the fake Combine-O-Tron 2000.

Meanwhile, George and Harold were running with all their might back to the library, carrying the *real* Combine-O-Tron 2000.

"That was SO easy!" laughed George.

"Yeah!" said Harold. "We sure got lucky this time!"

But when they reached the library door, George and Harold discovered that they hadn't been quite so lucky after all.

CHAPTER 14
MISS SINGERBRAINS

"What the heck is going on here?" shouted Miss Singerbrains. "I just got back from the restroom and found a *portable potty* in my library!"

"Harold!" said George. "Zap her with the Forgetcha-thingy—quick!"

"Nobody's zapping anybody with anything!" shouted Miss Singerbrains. She grabbed the Forgetchamacallit 2000 out of Harold's hands and yanked the Combine-O-Tron 2000 out of George's hands.

"I'm taking these things to the police right now!" she said. "Maybe they can sort this mess out!"

Miss Singerbrains marched downstairs to the parking lot, got in her car, and began driving to the police station.

"Well," said Harold, "we'll never catch up to her now!"

"Sure we will!" said George. "All we need are some *wings*!"

CHAPTER 15

65 MILLION YEARS BEFORE THE DAY BEFORE YESTERDAY

George and Harold grabbed a box of saltine crackers off of Miss Singerbrains's desk. Then the two friends stepped inside the Purple Potty and closed the door. Quickly, George reset the controls and pulled down on the chain.

A flash of green light lit up the room, and the Purple Potty vanished.

Suddenly, George and Harold were transported back in time to the late Cretaceous period of the Mesozoic era, a time when dinosaurs ruled the Earth.

Cautiously, George and Harold peeked out of the Purple Potty, which was now nestled precariously in the branches of a tall tree.

"Here chickie, chickie, chickie!" called George.

"Polly want a cracker?" called Harold as he tossed a handful of saltines into the air.

Suddenly, the two boys were swarmed by hungry pterodactyls.

Before long, a friendly-looking pterodactyl (a Quetzalcoatlus to be exact) swooped down and grabbed some crackers from Harold's hand.

"Aww, look," said Harold. "He likes me!"

"Great," said George. "Let's get him into the time machine and get out of here!"

Carefully, Harold took the pterodactyl in his arms and carried him into the Purple Potty. Then, the boys closed the door behind them, reset the controls, and pulled down on the chain.

Suddenly, George and Harold (and their new reptilian pal) were transported forward in time to the day before yesterday.

The door of the time machine swung open, and the three friends sailed out of the Purple Potty, through the library window, and up over the town.

George looked down on the city streets until finally he located Miss Singerbrains's car. "There she is!" George cried.

"I sure love our new pterodactyl," said Harold. "I'm gonna name him Crackers."

"Don't give him a name," said George. "We're not keeping him. We're just borrowing him!"

George, Harold, and Crackers swooped down and landed on Miss Singerbrains's car, which was parked at a traffic light.

Miss Singerbrains screamed in horror.

"Wait!" cried George. "There's no reason to be afraid. You're just *dreaming*!"

"I'm dreaming?" asked Miss Singerbrains.

"Sure. Think about it," said Harold. "Purple Potties appearing out of nowhere . . . kids running around with laser zappers . . . pterosaurs landing on your car . . . this stuff only happens in dreams."

"Gosh, you're right," said Miss Singerbrains. "But it all seems so real."

"Well, trust us," said George. "In a few minutes you won't remember any of it."

Before long, George, Harold, and Miss Singerbrains were all gliding back to school with their good pal Crackers. The Combine-O-Tron 2000 and the Forgetchamacallit 2000 were safe once again.

Soon, they arrived back at the library.

"I'll keep an eye on Miss Singerbrains," said George. "You take that pterodactyl back where we found him."

"Aww, can't we keep him?" asked Harold.

"No," said George sternly. "He belongs in his own time. Now take him back!"

"Aww, *maaaan*," said Harold.

Sadly, Harold carried Crackers into the
Purple Potty and closed the door. After a few
seconds, the time machine disappeared in
a flash of green light.

A half hour later, another flash of green light filled the room, and the Purple Potty was back.

"What took you so long?" asked George.

"Ummm . . . nothing," said Harold.

"Did you have any trouble taking Crackers back to his home?" asked George.

"Ummmm . . . not really," said Harold.

"You *DID* take him back to his home, didn't you?" asked George.

"Ummmmm . . . sure," said Harold, though he didn't *sound* very sure.

Quickly, George zapped Miss Singerbrains with the Forgetchamacallit 2000 and jumped into the Purple Potty. Then, with a quick flash of green light, they were gone.

CHAPTER 16

BACK TO THE PRESENT

Mr. Melvin was very happy to see his Purple Potty return to him . . . and even happier to see his beloved Combine-O-Tron 2000.

"Now all I need," he said with a sneer, "is to find Captain Underpants."

Fortunately, Captain Underpants (who you'll probably remember looked just like Melvin Sneedly) wasn't too far away. *Unfortunately*, he had spent the last two days getting himself into trouble.

First, he started off by annoying some old ladies. Captain Underpants had been helping them cross the street when he heard a little girl crying for her kitten, which was stuck in a tree.

Captain Underpants rescued the kitty but forgot about the old ladies.

"Hey!" shouted one of the old ladies. "That flying kid just left us up here in this tree!"

"I'm gonna get that kid if it's the last thing I do!" said the other old lady.

Next, Captain Underpants was soaring
above the football field when he encountered
an unidentified flying object. It was made
of brown leather and had white stitching on
the side.

"Hmmm," said Captain Underpants. "This
could be a dangerous UFO!" He grabbed it
and flew down to the football field, where,
oddly, the school's football team was having
a big game.

"I don't want anybody to panic!" Captain Underpants shouted. "But I just captured this UFO. I'm going to take it to the moon, where it can be safely destroyed."

Suddenly, the players from the visiting team tackled Captain Underpants, which cost the home team fifty yards . . . and the game.

"That kid just made us lose our biggest game of the year!" shouted Mr. Meaner.

"I'm gonna get that kid if it's the last thing I do," snarled the quarterback.

Finally, Captain Underpants got on the bad side of some skateboarders in the park. He had politely pointed out the *No Skateboarding* signs, but the skateboarders refused to go away. So Captain Underpants had no choice but to snap their skateboards in half with his kung-fu kicking action.

Then it was spankings for everyone!

"Dude!" cried one of the skateboarders. "That little dude just, like, duded our dudeboards."

"Dude," said another skateboarder. "I'm gonna dude that dude if it's the last dude I dude!"

CHAPTER 17

THE BIG SWITCHEROONIE

Mr. Melvin ordered George and Harold to stick their heads out the window and call for Captain Underpants. Soon, the Waistband Warrior appeared.

Mr. Melvin welcomed the caped hero inside and asked him to pose for a photo.

"Why, I'd be delighted," said Captain Underpants.

"Great," said Mr. Melvin. "Put these clothes on and stand over there!"

At first, Captain Underpants was reluctant
to put on clothes, but he finally agreed.

Mr. Melvin, who had worked all afternoon
reconfiguring the Combine-O-Tron 2000,
pressed the start button, then ran and stood
beside Captain Underpants. Suddenly, two
glowing lasers began encoding the DNA of
the two subjects it was about to combine.

Then, a burst of brilliant gray light shot out of the Combine-O-Tron 2000 and formed a ball of energy between Captain Underpants and Mr. Melvin. They both slid together into the gray light and formed a giant glob of fleshy goo.

The newly reconfigured Combine-O-Tron 2000 then switched polarities and began the process of separating the two human elements. The gray ball of light slowly changed to a lovely shade of pink.

Suddenly, there was a blinding flash of light, a quick puff of smoke, and it was all over. Everybody's brains were back where they belonged.

"Wow, that sure is a weird camera," said Captain Underpants (who now looked exactly like Captain Underpants). "Can I take these clothes off now? They're bad for my image."

"Go right ahead," said Melvin Sneedly (who now looked exactly like Melvin Sneedly).

Finally, it looked as if everything was back to normal. But as we all know, looks can be deceiving.

CHAPTER 18

THE RETURN OF THE RIDICULOUS ROBO-BOOGERS

Just then, the POOPSIE space shuttle landed at Piqua International Airport. It wasn't the smoothest of landings, due to the fact that three robotic boogers had just eaten most of the shuttle's tailfin and nearly all of its rocket thrusters.

Major Tomski and his crew had barely escaped with their lives.

Inside the school library, Captain
Underpants heard the astronauts' panicked
cries coming from the airport.

"This looks like a job for me!" he shouted.
And with a mighty "Tra-La-Laaaaa!", he
leaped out the window . . .

. . . and fell three stories to the ground.

George and Harold screamed and ran downstairs.

"Captain Underpants!" cried George. "Are you O.K.?"

"Speak to us!" cried Harold.

Captain Underpants slowly lifted his head in confusion.

"Mommy . . ." he said weakly, ". . . my train went swimming in the piano."

115

Meanwhile, over at Piqua International Airport, Carl, Trixie, and Frankenbooger had just finished eating the space shuttle and were now starting to munch on the control tower. The three globby gluttons grew bigger and bigger with every enormous bite.

"C'mon, Captain Underpants," cried George. "You've gotta save those people!"

"But I forgot how to fly," Captain Underpants said sheepishly.

"You didn't forget," laughed Melvin Sneedly, who was now floating above their heads. "You've just LOST your super powers. But don't worry, they've been safely transferred into *MY* body. Now *I'm* the world's greatest superhero!"

"Melvin," cried George, "those Robo-Boogers came back to Earth! They're attacking people at the airport! You've gotta help those people!"

"I'm not doing a thing until you guys change that comic book!" Melvin said. "And you better make me look cool this time!"

"But there's no time," cried Harold. "Those people need your help NOW!"

"Well, you better start drawing then, art boy!" said Melvin.

CHAPTER 19

NEVER UNDERESTIMATE THE POWER OF UNDERWEAR

George and Harold begged Melvin to use his super powers to save the day, but Melvin continued to refuse. Finally, Captain Underpants stepped in.

"You may have taken away my super powers," the Waistband Warrior said, "but I still have the power of underwear on my side. And nobody can take that away from me!"

Captain Underpants turned and ran toward the airport.

"Melvin," cried George frantically, "if you don't do something, those boogers are gonna *kill* Mr. Krupp!"

"That's not *my* fault," said Melvin. "You're the ones who wrote that stupid comic book about me. Now change it, or ELSE!"

George and Harold looked at each other. Their choice was simple: either fight with Captain Underpants (and probably die), or give in to the dark side and live.

The two boys turned and ran to the airport.

CHAPTER 20
BOOGER BRUNCH

George and Harold quickly caught up with
Captain Underpants. Soon, they were all at
the airport witnessing the carnage of the
Ridiculous Robo-Boogers.

Captain Underpants shouted out
a triumphant "Tra-La-Laaaaa!" from below.
Suddenly, the three Robo-Boogers turned
toward the familiar-sounding voice. Quickly,
their laser-guided eyeballs zoomed in on
three of the heroes who had made their lives
so miserable back in chapter 1. Immediately,
the Robo-Boogers leaped at George, Harold,
and Captain Underpants . . . and the chase
was on . . . again!

CHAPTER 21
CORNERED

The Robo-Boogers continued chasing
George, Harold, and Captain Underpants,
until at last the three frightened friends
were cornered at a local shopping center.

In a desperate attempt to save themselves, the three brave heroes began taking items from the outside sales bins and throwing them at the snarling beasts.

George grabbed a pair of low-fat tennis shoes and tossed them at Trixie. Trixie gobbled them up.

Harold found a delicious tube of wild-cherry-flavored hemorrhoid ointment and flung it at Frankenbooger.

Frankenbooger swallowed it whole.

RYTHING
XCEPT
SOFTENER
R NON-FABRIC SOFTENING NEEDS

SALE

Captain Underpants picked up a
genetically-modified, organic-orange-
flavored orange and chucked it at Carl.
Carl chewed it up with a smug grin.

Suddenly, Carl's laser eyes grew incredibly large. The haughty smile on his face turned into a panicked gasp as the wet, gooshy snot that covered his body began to dry up and crumble. Huge, crispy booglets shot off of his smoldering robotic endoskeleton like green popcorn.

"What's going on?" cried Harold.

"It's the *oranges*!" cried George. "It's gotta be the vitamin C in these oranges. It's combatting the cold and flu that caused those boogers to turn evil!"

Carl thrashed around brutally as more and more of his disintegrating body cracked off and fell to the ground. Finally, the lights in his panic-stricken laser eyes slowly went out. He stumbled over and crashed horribly into the parking lot. Carl—was dead.

CHAPTER 22

VITAMIN C YOU LATER

George, Harold, and Captain Underpants quickly began chucking oranges at Trixie and Frankenbooger. But the two remaining Robo-Boogers had gotten wise to the power of vitamin C. They ducked, jumped, dodged, and darted, doing whatever they could to avoid being hit by the deadly oranges.

"Hey! I've got an idea," said Captain Underpants. He grabbed two crates of oranges and ran off, while George and Harold continued flinging fruit ferociously.

"Where does he think *he's* going?" said George.

"I don't know," said Harold, "but his idea better work. We're running out of oranges!"

Soon, George and Harold were down to their last two oranges. They threw them as hard as they could, but alas, the potent projectiles missed their terrifying targets.

Trixie and Frankenbooger grabbed George and Harold and dangled them above their gigantic mouths.

"Well," said George, "it looks like this is the end."

"Yep," said Harold. "It was nice knowing you, pal."

Suddenly, the Robo-Boogers heard a familiar "Tra-La-Laaaaa!" coming from some-where over on the next page.

The repulsive Robo-Boogers dropped George and Harold, and stomped over to page 130. There they found Captain Underpants standing at the top of a large novelty toilet on the roof of John's House of Toilets. He was shouting, "Tra-La-Laaaaa!" and doing a very annoying dance, which made the Robo-Boogers very, very angry.

JOHN'S HOUSE OF TOILETS

WE'LL BOWL YOU OVER!

CHAPTER 23

THE UNDERPANTS DANCE (IN FLIP-O-RAMA™)

You've tried the Twist,
mastered the Macarena,
and figured out
the Funky Chicken. . . .

Now it's time to learn the most
annoying dance ever:
the Underpants Dance.

It's sure to irritate parents,
teachers, evil villains,
and kids of all ages!

Just follow the easy steps
in this chapter, and learn
the Underpants Dance today!!!

PILKEY® BRAND
O·RAMA

HERE'S HOW IT WORKS!

STEP 1

First, place your *left* hand inside the dotted lines marked "LEFT HAND HERE." Hold the book open *flat*.

STEP 2

Grasp the *right-hand* page with your right thumb and index finger (inside the dotted lines marked "RIGHT THUMB HERE").

STEP 3

Now *quickly* flip the right-hand page back and forth until the picture appears to be *animated*.

FLIP-O-RAMA 1

(pages 135 and 137)

Remember, flip *only* page 135.
While you are flipping, be sure you
can see the picture on page 135
and the one on page 137.
If you flip quickly, the two
pictures will start to look like
<u>one</u> *animated* picture.

For extra fun, try humming
a stupid song and flipping to the beat!

LEFT HAND HERE

STEP 1:
THE WEDGIE
WIGGLE

135

RIGHT
THUMB
HERE

136

STEP 1:
THE WEDGIE
WIGGLE

FLIP-O-RAMA 2

(pages 139 and 141)

Remember, flip *only* page 139.
While you are flipping, be sure you
can see the picture on page 139
and the one on page 141.
If you flip quickly, the two
pictures will start to look like
<u>one</u> *animated* picture.

For extra fun, try humming
a stupid song and flipping to the beat!

LEFT HAND HERE

STEP 2:
THE TOILET-TOP TANGO

139

RIGHT
THUMB
HERE

STEP 2:
THE TOILET-TOP
TANGO

FLIP-O-RAMA 3

(pages 143 and 145)

Remember, flip *only* page 143.
While you are flipping, be sure you
can see the picture on page 143
and the one on page 145.
If you flip quickly, the two
pictures will start to look like
<u>one</u> *animated* picture.

For extra fun, try humming
a stupid song and flipping to the beat!

LEFT HAND HERE

STEP 3:
THE WAISTBAND
WATUSI

RIGHT
THUMB
HERE

STEP 3:
THE WAISTBAND
WATUSI

FLIP-O-RAMA 4

(pages 147 and 149)

Remember, flip *only* page 147.
While you are flipping, be sure you
can see the picture on page 147
and the one on page 149.
If you flip quickly, the two
pictures will start to look like
<u>one</u> *animated* picture.

For extra fun, try humming
a stupid song and flipping to the beat!

LEFT HAND HERE

STEP 4:
THE BIG BUTT
BOOGIE

RIGHT
THUMB
HERE

STEP 4:
THE BIG BUTT
BOOGIE

CHAPTER 24
SQUISHIES, PART 2

Trixie and Frankenbooger had seen enough.
They couldn't stand to watch Captain
Underpants doing that stupid dance one
second longer. So they pushed down on
the seat of the large novelty toilet to hoist
themselves up on the roof.

Unfortunately for Trixie and Frankenbooger, they had been so irritated by the Underpants Dance that they hadn't noticed the two crates of oranges placed carefully under the gigantic toilet seat. When they pressed down, the pressure of the toilet seat crushed the orange crates, spraying delicious, vitaminey orange juice all over their big, bad, boogery bodies.

George, Harold, and Captain Underpants watched as their monstrous archenemies began decomposing before their very eyes.

"What happened to them?" asked Harold.

"I gave them a *Squishy*," said Captain Underpants. "It's the latest fad."

The Robo-Boogers jerked around wildly as the quickly drying snot crumbled off of their smoking robotic endoskeletons. Then, after a few minutes of spinning and screaming, they slowly tumbled to the ground in two metallic heaps.

Trixie and Frankenbooger—were dead.

CHAPTER 25

"BIG MELVIN"

Soon, Ingrid Ashley from Channel 4 Eyewitness News arrived at the scene. "How did you manage to destroy the Robo-Boogers?" she asked.

"I'll answer that," said Melvin Sneedly, as he swooped in front of the cameras. He was robed in some old drapes that he had tied around his neck at the last minute, and he looked quite silly.

"I, *Big Melvin*, fought those monsters with my mighty super powers," Melvin fibbed. "Then I destroyed them with my super-smart brain!"

"No, you didn't," said Harold.

"You weren't even here!" said George.

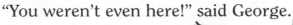

"Don't listen to those guys," said Melvin. "I, *Big Melvin*, am the real hero here." Melvin flew above the two defeated Robo-Boogers and used his new laser eye-beams to burn the letters *B* and *M* in front of the dead creatures.

"Just like Zorro," said Big Melvin, "I shall sign my initials on all of my heroic handi-work. From now on, whenever you see a big *BM*, you'll think of me!"

"That's funny," said George. "Big *BM*s have always made me think of you."

Big Melvin flew over to Captain
Underpants and grabbed him by the arm.

"Now," said Big Melvin, "the entire world
shall bear witness to the humiliating defeat
of Captain Underpants!"

Suddenly, George and Harold got an idea.
They turned and ran back to the school while
Big Melvin continued to threaten Captain
Underpants.

"I command you to bow down to me,"
shouted Big Melvin.

"Never!" said Captain Underpants.

"You SHALL bow down to me!" Big
Melvin yelled.

"I SHAN'T!" cried Captain Underpants.

"Then," said Big Melvin, as he untied the
drapes around his neck, "you will feel the
power of my wrath!"

CHAPTER 26
THE DRAPES OF WRATH

Big Melvin held his drapes tightly, then
smacked Captain Underpants in the tushie
with them.

"I command you to deny underwear and
accept the power of Big Melvin!" he shouted.

"No *way, Pedro*!" cried Captain Underpants.

Big Melvin smacked Captain Underpants
again.

"Bow down to me," he commanded, "and I shall spare your life!"

"Aww, go jump off a duck!" said Captain Underpants defiantly.

Suddenly, George and Harold returned to the scene, out of breath, and hiding something behind their backs.

"Hey, Big Melvin!" shouted George, huffing and puffing.

"What?" yelled Big Melvin.

Harold pulled the Combine-O-Tron 2000 out from behind his back and aimed it at Melvin and Captain Underpants.

"You shouldn't leave your toys lyin' around in the library, bub!" he said slyly.

Melvin shrieked in horror as Harold pulled the trigger.

BLAZZZZT!

A blinding flash of gray light shot out of the Combine-O-Tron 2000, surrounding Melvin and Captain Underpants and squishing them together.

George had reset the controller to combine them both, transfer the super powers back to Captain Underpants, then separate them.

"I sure hope this works," said Harold.

"Me, too," said George.

CHAPTER 27

TO MAKE A LONG STORY SHORT

It did.

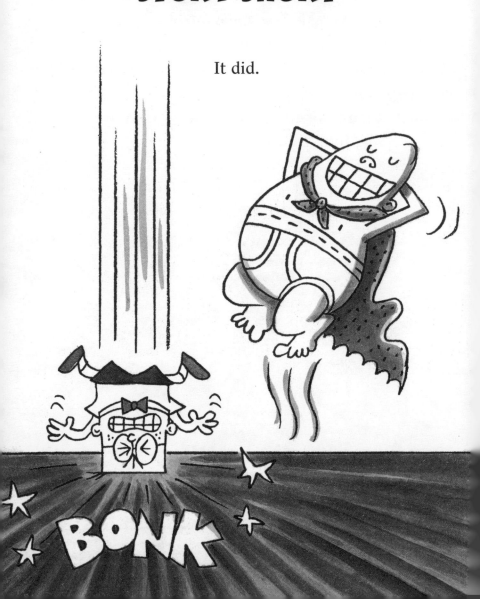

CHAPTER 28

WITH BIG UNDERWEAR COMES BIG RESPONSIBILITY

Big Melvin fell to the ground with a thud. Immediately, Captain Underpants began floating in the air.

"Hey!" cried the good Captain. "I've got my super powers back! I knew that underwear would never let me down!"

George turned and zapped the Channel 4 Eyewitness News team with the Forgetchamacallit 2000.

FLASH!

Suddenly, the Channel 4 Eyewitness News team (as well as everyone at home watching the story unfold on Channel 4 Eyewitness News) immediately forgot what had just happened.

The horror was over, everything was back to normal, and everyone was happy.

Well . . . everyone except Big Melvin, that is.

"*Waaaaaah!*" sobbed Melvin. "I want my super powers back!"

"Aww, quit your whining, bub!" said George. "You've been a total jerk for the last two books. You should just be happy that you didn't get your comeuppance!"

CHAPTER 29

COMEUPPANCE
SEE ME SOMETIME

Soon, a crowd gathered and began to
recognize Melvin.

"Hey!" cried Miss Anthrope. "That's the
little squirt who said he was going to fire
my *hiney*!"

"There he is!" shouted a couple of very angry old ladies. "That's the little brat who left us up in a tree."

"He made us lose the big game," cried the entire football team simultaneously.

"Dudes," yelled one of the skateboarders, "that's the little dude who duded our dude-boards a few dudes ago!"

"Heh, heh," laughed Melvin nervously. "Maybe I'll just go home now."

"*Get him!*" shouted the old ladies.

"AAAAAH!" screamed Melvin as he ran away, followed closely by a large group of very angry people.

CHAPTER 30
HAROLD'S SURPRISE

As Melvin and his angry mob ran off into the sunset, George and Harold had just one last thing to deal with.

A quick squirt of water to Captain Underpants's face was all it took to bring him back to his Kruppy old self.

"Well, that takes care of that," said George, and the two boys walked back to their tree house.

As George climbed up the ladder to the
tree house, Harold became quite fidgety.

"Ummmmmm . . . " said Harold nervously,
"there's something I should probably tell
you, George."

But when George reached the top of
the ladder and looked inside the tree house,
no explanation was necessary.

"Hey!" said George. "I thought you told me you took Crackers back to his home."

"I did," said Harold. "Back to his *new* home."

"*Harold*," said George sternly, "we can't keep a pet pterodactyl. Do you know how many crackers they need to eat every day? We could never afford it."

"I know. . . . " said Harold sadly. "But look how cute he is. And he's made friends with Sulu, too. Can't we keep him for just one night?"

"Well, alright," said George. "But we're taking him back tomorrow."

CHAPTER 31
TOMORROW

The next day, George, Harold, and Sulu returned to school with Crackers tucked snugly into Harold's book bag. Together, the four friends sneaked back upstairs to the library, where the Purple Potty stood before them in all its forbidden glory.

"Come on," said George. "Let's give this baby another spin."

"I don't know," said Harold. "Maybe we should give it a day to cool off."

"Nah, I'm sure it can be used two days in a row," said George. "What could possibly go wrong?"

"But didn't Melvin warn us not to use this machine two days in a row?" asked Harold.

"Yeah," said George. "Back in chapter 12, starting with the first word in the third line of the second paragraph on page 77."

"What exactly did he say?" asked Harold.

"Beats me," said George. "I'm not very good at remembering details."

"Well, I don't know about this," said Harold. "What if our journey brings about the end of the world as we know it?"

"That's ridiculous," said George. "It all sounds like a setup for the sequel to a really lame children's book!"

The four friends stepped inside the Purple
Potty and closed the door behind them.
George set the controller to return them to
the Cretaceous period of the Mesozoic era
and then pulled the chain.

Suddenly, an orange light began flashing
wildly.

"Hey! I don't remember seeing an orange
light before," said Harold.

Then the Purple Potty began to shake
and rock violently.

"I don't remember this thing shaking
and rocking before, either," said George.

"Something is wrong!" cried Harold.
"Something is terribly, *terribly* wrong!"

Suddenly, the entire room lit up with an explosive burst of lightning, and the Purple Potty began to disappear into a whirlwind of electric air.

The only thing that could be heard above the chaotic clatter was the sound of two terrified voices screaming into the unknown abyss.

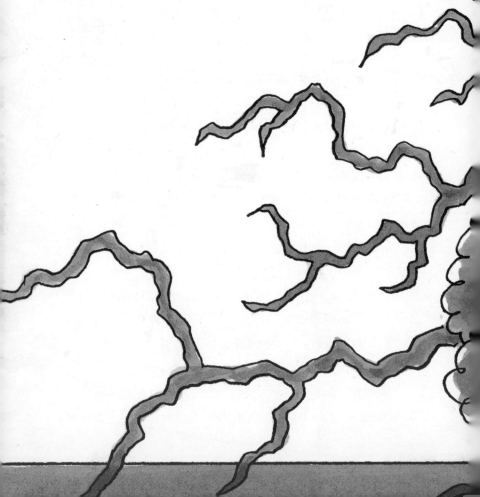

"Oh, NO!" screamed one of the voices.
"HERE WE GO AGAIN!" screamed
the other.